The Goffins

Lofty and Eave

ALSO IN THIS SERIES

Fun and Games

The Goffins
Lofty and Eave

JEANNE WILLIS
illustrated by Nick Maland

WALKER
BOOKS

For my dear friend Jimmy Scar
J.W.

For Melanie, Adrian and Florence, with love
N.M.

First published 2009 by Walker Books Ltd
87 Vauxhall Walk, London SE11 5HJ

2 4 6 8 10 9 7 5 3

Text © 2009 Jeanne Willis
Illustrations © 2009 Nick Maland

This book has been typeset in ITC Veljovic

Printed and bound in Great Britain by Clays Ltd, St Ives plc

British Library Cataloguing in Publication Data:
a catalogue record for this book is available from the British Library

ISBN 978-1-4063-0869-3

www.walker.co.uk

CONTENTS

THE CARRUTHERS

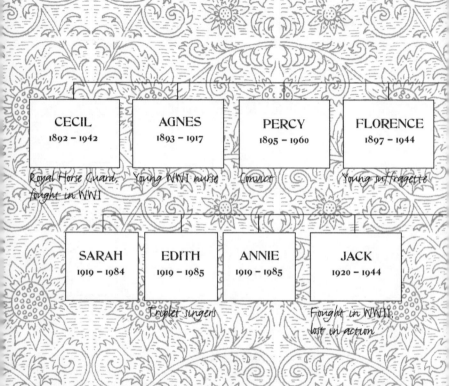

CECIL	AGNES	PERCY	FLORENCE
1892 – 1942	1893 – 1917	1895 – 1960	1897 – 1944

Royal Horse Guard, fought in WWI

Young WWI nurse

Convict

Young suffragette

SARAH	EDITH	ANNIE	JACK
1919 – 1984	1919 – 1985	1919 – 1985	1920 – 1944

Triplet singers

Fought in WWII lost in action

FAMILY TREE

MONTAGUE CARRUTHERS
1870 – 1960
m
MAUD GOODWIN
1871 – 1971

Explorer, sailor, whaling ship

Suffragette, Titanic, WWI Nurse, maid servant called Violet, lived to be 100

SID
1899 – 1975
m
DOLLY GRAY
1900 – 1975

Joined army to fight WWI, under age, lost leg, won medals

VICTORIA
1901 – 1904

GORDON
1922 – 2005
m
PEGGY ELLIS
1926 –

Fought against Hitler in WWII as a young man

MARY
1926 – 2006

FRANK
1928 – 2003

Evacuee

Evacuee

SIMON
1958 –

PHILLIP
1960 –
m
SUSAN DERBYSHIRE
1966 –

Saved child from drowning

GEORGE
1999 –

Discovered Goffins living in his grandma's attic

CHAPTER ONE

THROUGH THE GREEN DOOR

George never wanted to move to Grandma Peggy's in the first place. He told his parents this but they wouldn't listen. They don't when you're ten.

"It's a lovely old house," said Mum. "There's a big garden. Go and play in it, George. Now, George!"

But he had no one to play with. The best games were impossible to enjoy on his own.

Football? It was no fun scoring goal after goal when there was no goalie, no one to tackle and no one to cheer when you were forty nil up. Where was the competition in that?

Hide-and-seek was hopeless; there was no one to find him. He could hide in the shed behind a bag of manure for days without being found. He was too old to play that anyway.

Cops and robbers? If he was the robber, there was no one to catch him. If he was a cop, there was no one to chase. Pointless. Useless. Boring.

It was the summer holidays. George hadn't had a chance to make new friends and his parents hadn't had a chance to make him a new brother or sister. The excuse was that they were too busy looking after Grandma. It was so selfish of them.

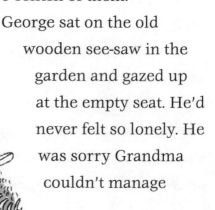

George sat on the old wooden see-saw in the garden and gazed up at the empty seat. He'd never felt so lonely. He was sorry Grandma couldn't manage on her own but in his darkest moments he wished she'd never been born. His parents never had time for him any more. He was bored stiff but when he told them that, they told him to go and keep Grandma company.

George hardly knew Grandma. He'd only met her twice in his life. Even then he hadn't spoken to her because he'd been a baby. What did eighty-year-old grandmas like to talk about? He had no idea. George's train of thought was interrupted by his mum, who was striding across the lawn calling his name.

"George!"

"What now?" he muttered.

"I'm making Grandma a cup of tea. Take these biscuits in to her, would you?" She passed George a basket with a fancy-looking handle.

George sighed wearily, then he took the basket and sloped indoors to the back room which overlooked the garden.

Lofty and Eave

Grandma's bed was in there because she couldn't manage the stairs. Feeling shy, he knocked and went in.

"Whadda those?" Grandma snapped, scowling at him.

"Biscuits."

"I don't like *those* biscuits. I told them I don't like the jam ones but nobody listens. They don't when you're eighty. You'll find that out one day, boy."

George stared out of the window. The silence grew longer and longer.

"Don't say much, do you?" she grumbled.

George tried desperately to think of something to talk about.

"I like your dressing gown," he said.

Grandma ignored him and tried to switch on the TV with her mobile phone. She pointed it angrily at the screen, jabbing at the buttons with her shaky fingers.

"Now that's broken," she groaned. "Stupid thing. It's too fiddly. Why can't I just have a normal telly that goes on and off like they used to?"

George picked up the remote control, which had fallen on the floor.

"You're meant to use this, Grandma."

She tutted and threw the phone into her handbag.

"Mobiles," she muttered. "I didn't want one, but they said I had to. I never use it. Who am I going to phone? All my chums are dead."

George wasn't really listening. He'd tuned into his favourite cartoon, the one he always used to watch at his old house with his best mates, Warren, Dino and Jermaine. They all thought it was hilarious, but Grandma didn't. She folded her arms and harrumphed.

"I'm not watching this rubbish. I want to see the snooker."

"Yeah, just a sec," said George.

George hated watching snooker so he didn't

change channels straight away. He didn't think Grandma would mind if he watched his programme for a bit.

But she did. She minded very much. She glared at him, her eyes scarily magnified by the thick lenses in her glasses.

"You've got a nerve, boy! Coming in here and watching my telly. This is my house and I'm watching the snooker."

Reluctantly, George handed her the remote and pulled a face behind her back. What she'd just said about it being her house had really annoyed him.

"It's not just your house," he said. "I live here too, don't I?"

"Fat lot of choice I had in the matter," spluttered Grandma.

George took it that she didn't want him living there at all. He felt hurt and angry when he thought of everything he'd had to give up for her sake.

15

Lofty and Eave

"I never wanted to live here in the first place, you know," he snapped. "I hate it. I've got no friends, I've got nothing to do and it's ALL YOUR FAULT!"

"George!"

His mother was standing in the doorway holding Grandma's cup of tea. She'd heard every word.

"How dare you say such horrid things to Grandma?"

"I didn't mean it," said George, but it was obvious he had so she sent him to bed. It was only half past six. Even babies didn't go to bed at half past six.

George ran up the three flights of stairs that led to his room and slammed the door. He threw himself onto his bed and punched his pillow. Then he rolled onto his back and repeated all the rude words he'd learnt at his old school in London. When he'd run out of rude words, he invented even ruder ones to describe his parents.

He must have sworn himself to sleep, because when he woke up, it was dark. He could see the moon through the slanted window in the high, sloping ceiling. His bedroom had been built into the left-hand side of the attic, facing Grandma's front garden.

17

It was L-shaped and very small because the larger space under the eaves had never been converted.

That part of the loft faced the back garden and, according to his father, it was used for storing junk and had been since the house was built in Victorian times. The only way in was through a small green door opposite George's bed, but he'd been banned from exploring.

"It could be dangerous," his father had said. "Poisonous substances, sharp objects, rats ... who knows? No one's been in there for years."

But if that was true, where was that voice coming from? It was very faint but it sounded just like a little girl laughing. It seemed to be coming from behind the green door. George sat up, aware that his heart was thumping. He held his breath and listened... Silence. He must have imagined it. He was about to lie back down when he heard it again – girlish laughter!

Maybe it was a ghost. His mum had told him that in Victorian times, his bedroom was used by servants. Maybe this was the ghost of a little servant girl. But then he heard soft footsteps. Ghosts didn't make noises when they walked, did they?

He slipped off his trainers, got off the bed and tiptoed over to the door as quietly as he could. He'd almost reached it when suddenly he trod on a loose floorboard.

19

Lofty and Eave

It creaked loudly and to his enormous shock, he heard another voice coming from the loft. This time, it was low and gruff. There was a man in there too! George would have been frightened, but the man sounded a lot more scared than he was.

"Hark, Littley!" whispered the man. "Whyfor be yonder door a-screaking?"

George pressed his ear against the door just in time to hear the little girl reply.

"'Tis oh-nee the westerly wind a-blowing through the sky-like, Pappy."

She didn't sound the slightest bit worried. George's mind was racing. Why did they speak in such a strange, old-fashioned way? At first he thought they might be refugees, but they weren't speaking in a foreign language; he'd understood every word. The girl had called the man "Pappy" which was like Papa. They must be father and daughter – he was convinced of that – but where had they come from and what on earth were they doing in there?

He heard more padded footsteps followed by the dull thump of the skylight shutting inside the attic. He knew he wasn't dreaming because his dreams were always dull and this was exciting.

George wondered for a depressing moment if he might have got it all wrong and that the voices were coming from the house next door, but it seemed unlikely. Grandma's house was detached. It was several metres away from the next building – it would have been impossible for the sound of someone whispering to travel that far.

There was no doubt about it – there were people hiding in the loft. Overwhelmed by curiosity, George crouched down and tried to peer through a tiny crack near the bottom of the door where one of the wooden panels had shrunk slightly. He held his eyelids wide open but he couldn't see anyone – it was too dark. With a sigh, he straightened up – but he did it too quickly and cracked the top of his head on the brass doorknob.

The pain was excrutiating. George shoved his fist in his mouth to stifle the yell – but too late. He'd been heard.

CHAPTER TWO

"I SURRENDER!"

It was now perfectly clear to whoever was in the loft that the stifled yell was not caused by the westerly wind; someone had discovered them. George could hear them whispering urgently to each other, then the skylight creaked open. Worried that they were trying to escape out of the window, he tapped on the door politely.

"Hello? I just want to make friends."

There was no reply, so he tried again.

"I won't hurt you. I'm only a kid and I'm really weedy."

That was his nickname at school: Weedy G.

Nobody meant it nastily. He wasn't particularly weak or small. It was just that the friends he used to hang round with were unusually well-built for their age, especially Jermaine. Compared to Jermaine, George felt like a different species and he was slightly afraid of him. He hated that feeling and he was sorry that he'd frightened the people in the loft. If only they could see him, he felt sure it would put their minds at rest.

"Don't be afraid," he said. "Open the door ... please?"

The girl sounded much braver than her father. George could hear her trying to reassure him.

"Himself be a peacefun littley, like myneself," she insisted. "Open yonder door, Pappy!" But he refused.

"Us darst not, Littley! Himself be bringin' mischeef and misery!"

As kind words had failed, George tried to bribe them instead.

"If you let me in, I'll fetch you some biscuits ... with jam."

There was a long pause.

"With jam, Pappy!" exclaimed the girl, but he still wouldn't open the door so she started sobbing to get her own way.

"Myneself be so a-loney, Pappy – uf-uf-uf – so a-loney!"

"Oh ... welly well," he sighed.

Someone was struggling to draw back a large, rusty bolt on the inside of green door. George waited for a few seconds.

"All right if I come in now?"

No one answered, so he gave the door a push. It seemed to be stuck, so he followed it up with a hard shove. The door flew open and he fell headfirst into the loft, landing flat on his face on a bearskin rug. Somebody giggled but there was no one to be seen.

Above him, hanging from the rafters on a long chain, was a big, brass chandelier. It held twelve lumpy candles which lit the loft with

a soft amber glow. George got to his knees
and looked around in amazement.

The loft had been divided into rooms
separated by large pieces of furniture. He
guessed he must be in the sitting room – there
was a mantelpiece with a stuffed crocodile
basking on the hearth. Next to this was a
battered chaise longue and a low, wooden
table carved with bun feet. To his right was

a heavy bookshelf filled with musty medical
books, recipe books, atlases, encyclopedias,
diaries, journals and row upon row of
photograph albums.

The wall nearest the door was stacked
to the roof with old trunks and boxes, all of
which had been carefully labelled in the same
childish handwriting. He read the nearest
ones out loud.

There was still no sign of anybody though. George stood up in the hope that he'd spot them hiding in the gloom. Hundreds of eyes stared back at him. On every wall, someone had hung portraits and photographs of men, women and children from several generations. Some were in fancy, gilt frames, others were tattered and faded and simply pinned to the beams. He had no idea who these people were, but somehow they seemed vaguely familiar.

Directly in front of him there was a black and white photo of a bride and groom. George picked it up and studied it. In pencil, on the back, someone had scribbled "Gordon and Peggy Carruthers" – they were his grandparents! He'd never known his grandpa and had only ever seen Grandma as an old person. This wedding photo made him realize with a jolt that they had been young once.

Somebody stifled a cough behind him. George span round and came face to face

with a man in a tremendous plumed helmet astride a stallion. It was only a portrait but it was almost life-sized and it made him jump. He felt even more peculiar when he read the title at the bottom of the frame.

**CECIL CARRUTHERS,
ROYAL HORSEGUARDS, 1914**

Carruthers? That was George's surname. The hairs on his neck stood up. Next to this portrait was another one, featuring a sailor fighting a ferocious polar bear on an ice floe. This also had a title.

Montague Carruthers, 1891

Flicking
his eyes
between
the sailor
and the
horseguard,
it struck
George that
they must
be related.
There was a
very strong

family likeness. But not only did Cecil and
Montague look like each other, they also
looked like him, only older and with luxurious
moustaches.

As George stepped back, absorbing the
fact that these heroic figures were none other
than his ancient relatives, he almost fell over
an artist's easel. It was propping up a small
oil painting of a lady in crinolines perched
on a purple chaise longue reading a book to

a child. He had no idea who
the woman was but the
furniture seemed familiar.
Where had he seen that
antique sofa before?

George racked his
brains then, with a
start, he realized he was
standing right next to it.
It hadn't been obvious straight away because
it had faded from deep purple to pale lilac and
burst its horsehair stuffing.

He'd just sat down on it to gather his
thoughts when, without warning, a tiny girl
with wild, red hair leapt out from behind.

"Halloo, Himself!" she said, grinning from
ear to ear.

George shot out of his seat. The girl clapped
her hands over her mouth and giggled, fixing
him with small, bright eyes the colour of
gooseberries. She was so short, she barely
came up to his chest.

Lofty and Eave

She was wearing the oddest outfit; an Easter bonnet the size of a dustbin lid covered in blue ribbons, a pair of droopy vintage knickerbockers and a white dress made from layer upon layer of netting which looked very similar to the one in Grandma Peggy's wedding photo.

The clothes were all far too big for her. She'd managed to belt the dress in and she'd chopped it off at the knee but she still looked like a fairy drowning in blancmange.

"Halloo ... you?" said George.

He wasn't sure what to call her. She
curtseyed and shook his hand.

"Myneself be called Eave," she said.
"Whatfor does yourself be called?"

"I be called – I'm George."

She wrinkled her freckled nose and
mimicked the way he said his name.

"Jowge? Yourself be a Lundiner, yay?"

"Yeah," he said. "I lived there all my life
until now." It made him miserable just
thinking about it.

Eave looked him up and down.

"How old be yourself?" she asked.

He told her he was nearly eleven. Eave
stood on her tiptoes. "Myneself be nine whole
summers," she boasted.

She looked younger, but right now her age
was hardly at the front of George's mind.

"What on earth are you doing in my
grandma's attic?" he asked.

Eave put her hands on her hips and called
for her father in a theatrical whisper.

"Pappy? Come hither, Pappy! Say halloo to Jowge."

It seemed as if he'd never come out of hiding but finally he plucked up courage and shuffled out of the shadows. He was the same height as George – which was short for a fully grown man –, but he seemed taller because he was wearing a horseguard's helmet decorated with a magnificent scarlet plume.

"'Tis yak hair!" he announced.

He was also wearing patched breeches and sealskin slippers which looked suspiciously like the ones worn by the sailor in the polar bear painting. He stepped forward to introduce himself.

"Halloo, Jowge. Myneself be called Lofty."

He bowed deeply. The helmet fell off, missed the bearskin rug and crashed to the floor, rolling and bouncing like a saucepan.

"Alack!" wailed Eave, shushing the helmet frantically. "Great-Great Uncool Cecil's brain-lid hath be-fallen!"

For a second, George didn't understand what she was talking about, then it dawned on him.

"Uncool Cecil? Oh, you mean *Uncle* Cecil! He's the horseguard in that portrait, right?"

He turned to point at it but when he looked back, Lofty and Eave had vanished.

"Where are you?" he whispered. "Why are you hiding?"

A small voice hissed at him from inside a wardrobe.

"Shhhh! If Them Below did hear the fearfill clangerin', us will be cotched!"

Unfortunately, someone down below had heard the noise. It was George's father. He was half whispering, half shouting from the bottom stairwell trying not to wake up Grandma.

"George, is that you crashing about?"

Now he was making his way up the stairs. With his heart in his mouth, George scrambled out of the attic and back through the green door. He'd just closed it behind him when his dad came in. He didn't sound very pleased.

"What's all the noise? What have you broken this time? It's the middle of the night!"

George shrugged.

"Nothing. My bedside lamp. It just fell."

It wasn't broken. Even so, his father insisted on checking the bulb and examining the flex.

"Lamps don't just fall. What did you do? You want to watch your temper. Mum said you lost it with Grandma earlier."

George slumped on his bed miserably.

"I said I was sorry."

His father sat down next to him and George knew he was in for a lecture.

"I know moving here hasn't been easy for you, George," he said, "but it's not easy for any of us and it would help enormously if you would stop being so —"

A distant squeak stopped him mid-sentence. His eyes darted to the green door and he frowned. George tried to distract him.

"If I stopped being so ... what, Dad?'

His father walked over to the green door and pressed his ear against it.

"I heard a squeak," he said. "We must have rats in the attic."

It must have been Eave – it was a girlish squeal, not a ratty one – but George could see how his father might have jumped to that conclusion.

"Oh, *that* squeak," he said. "That was me."

He slid his feet into his trainers and rubbed the soles against the floorboards, trying to produce a similar sound, but his father wasn't convinced.

"What I heard was a rat squeak," he said. "I'll have to get the rat catcher in."

"It's not rats," said George. "I'd have heard them before. I sleep here every night, so I should know. Can you hear them now?"

The attic was silent. But his father insisted that if it was a rat – or a squirrel – and it bit through a wire, it could cause a fire.

"I'll call pest control in the morning," he said. "Just to be on the safe side. Oh and George? Put your pyjamas on, son."

George waited until his father had gone back to bed, then he crept through the green door again.

"It's safe ... you can come out now," he called softly.

Eave popped up from inside a piano and Lofty materialized from behind the bookcase. He was aiming a harpoon straight at George's head.

"This deadly 'poon did belong to your Great- Great- Grandpappy Montague," he said. "Thus, himself did defeat the dreaded poleybear!"

"Hold fire, Pappy!"

41

begged Eave, "'Twill go off – *blam!* – and
Them Below will be cotchin' us!"

Not wishing them to be caught and because
he didn't fancy being shot, George put his
hands up.

"I surrender!"

Lofty lowered his weapon and fiddled
apologetically with the yak plume which had
flopped over his left eye.

"Us darst not be too carefree, Jowge," he
said. "Us does live in dread of being cotched."

"You nearly got caught just now!" said
George. "My father thinks you're rats. He
heard you from my bedroom."

"Myneself could not be helpin' it!" protested
Eave. "Pappy did tread on myne piggy." She
rubbed her little toe.

"'Twas be-accidents," mumbled Lofty.

"'Twas be-accidents that myneself did
skrike!" insisted Eave, stamping her foot.

The stamping wasn't loud but it was
enough to make Lofty panic. He put his hands

over his ears and instinctively rushed round on tiptoes looking for a new hiding place. Eave began shushing herself, her foot and her father who, in his frenzied attempt to keep quiet, was making more noise than ever.

"See how us does live in dread?" he mouthed.

"Then why are you living in Grandma's attic in the first place?" asked George.

The question stopped Lofty in his tracks and he sat down on the burst chaise longue with a far-away look in his eye.

"'Tis a long story," he sighed. "Yourself doesn't want to be hearin' old Lofty's ramblins."

"Yay himself does!" insisted Eave. "Doesn't you, Jowge?"

George wasn't about to argue. He sat down next to Eave and when they were sitting as comfortably as they could, Lofty began.

CHAPTER THREE

US BE GOFFINS

Lofty thought for a moment.

"Howfor shall myneself begin this sorrowfill tale?"

"Yourself must be beginnin' at the beginnin'," said Eave.

Lofty ummed and ahhed and chuckled softly to himself. He pulled at his chin and sighed and seemed so lost in his own memories, George thought the story would never be told, so he tried asking him a question to get things moving.

"Why you don't live in your own house, Lofty?"

Lofty and Eave

Lofty snapped out of his daydream, cleared his throat and said a very strange thing.

"A Goffin in his own house be rarer than a skylark down a rabbit hole."

"What's a Goffin?" asked George.

Lofty put his arm around Eave, adjusted his helmet and saluted.

"Us be Goffins."

With great pride, he told George that they came from an ancient race of forgotten people.

"Myne Great-Great-Great Grandpappy Steeple be borned on the isle of Inish Goff.

Oh-nee ten other fambilies did ever dwell there—"

"Us ancient rellies be called the Steeples and the Tilers," interrupted Eave.

Lofty scowled at her.

"Whoself be telling this tale, Littley?"

"Yourself!" Eave grinned. "Oh-nee don't be forgessing how, by and by, Inish Goff did sink into the Eye-Rush Sea!"

"The island sank!" exclaimed George. "No wonder I've never heard of it."

It hadn't sunk straight away, Lofty told him. It happened over many years.

Lofty and Eave

"Meantimes, it did become mighty boggy and brackish," he said. "Myne great grandplods did build dwellin's in trees where it be high and dry, but Inish Goff did keep sinking and sinking—"

"And the Eye-Rush Sea, it did keep risin' and risin'—" said Eave.

"Shush! Mynself does tell this betterly!" insisted Lofty. "The sea did keep risin' and the goodly soil be spoilt for crops and cattle and the sea did keep risin' and a-risin'..."

Eave slapped his knee playfully.

"Pappy! Yourself did tell that bit already. Myne greatly grandplods be a-starvin', Jowge. Thus, themselves did build rafts and sail away!"

Lofty folded his arms, pushed his helmet down over his eyes and sulked. George nudged Eave.

"You've upset him. He wanted to tell me that bit. Lofty? Did all the Goffins manage to escape before the island sank?"

Lofty didn't reply so George tapped him on the helmet in case he hadn't heard.

"Did they all escape, Lofty?"

He was about to answer when Eave butted in again.

"Some be drownded, Jowge!"

Her eyes filled with tears, then she grabbed his sweatshirt sleeve and blew her nose on it.

"Drownded!" she sniffed, "Myneself be – uf-uf – so – uf – sorryfill."

Lofty lifted up his helmet again and gave her a comforting squeeze.

"Come Littley, whyfor does yourself be skriking? Us Goffins did mostly survive!"

George was anxious to know what happened to the survivors. By all accounts, most had drifted to the Isle of Man, but the Tilers landed at the Mull of Galloway and the Steeples docked at Blackpool.

"Themselves did try to build Goffin dwellin's in trees," said Lofty. "But alack! The evil landymen did come with baying hounds—"

"Grrr!" growled Eave.

"Themselves did blunder myne ancient rellies with sticks and stones!" wailed Lofty.

"Boo!" hissed Eave. "Whyfor be yourself not booin', Jowge?"

She wanted him to join in with the hissing but George felt a bit self-conscious.

"Boo," he mumbled flatly.

Eave shook her head.

"Nay, Jowge, yourself must be booin' betterly than that! Say 'Booooooo!'"

She looked so funny, George forgot his inhibition and booed back at her – quietly, but with great gusto. Eave nodded approvingly.

"Yourself be doin' it much betterly, Jowge!"

They continued to boo at each other until Lofty had completely lost the plot.

51

"You were telling me about the landowners chasing the Goffins away," George reminded him. "Where did they go after that?"

"Themselves did dwell in caves a-times, but Goffins be used to living on high and did feel wary and be-wilbured down below."

And so Lofty told him how they had moved secretly into the towers of ruined castles and the belfries of crumbling churches and the tops of old windmills. Slowly the Goffin

population spread into the cities, setting up home in abandoned lofts and the top floors of condemned high-rise flats.

"Yourself be never more than five roofs away from a Goffin," said Eave.

George was amazed. When he'd lived in London, he must have been surrounded by Goffins and never known it.

"Not many does," said Lofty. "Gladly, Them Below be mostly iggerant of Goffins."

"But us be knowin' allsorts about your fambily, Jowge," Eave grinned. "Longways back to your great-great grandplods. Us be knowin' their hopes, dreams and secrets."

"How come?" he asked.

"Mynself does peek at their scribblin's and study the trove left in trunks, all of which is tellin' of peepil." Eave fiddled with the ribbons on her enormous bonnet. "This be your Great-Great-Grandmuppy Maud's sunbonny. Thus, myneself be knowing herself did have a greatly normous head."

George smiled.

"Are you sure you haven't just got a little head?"

Eave shook the bonnet so hard it fell over her eyes and she went silent, like a parrot who'd had a cloth thrown over its cage.

George adjusted it for her. He wasn't

the kind of boy to adjust a girl's hat, but he felt surprisingly protective towards this one.

"Thankly, Jowge. Yourself be a genteelman, like your Great-Great-Grandpappy Montague," she chirped.

"I didn't even know I had a Great-Great-Grandpa Montague until today," he confessed.

"Yourself does have his smile, Jowge," said Eave.

"Yes, but who was he? What did he do?" George had been wondering about Montague Carruthers ever since he'd seen his portrait.

"Himself be a famous explorer, Jowge," said Eave. "Us did find an ancient almanac belonging to himself, be-filled with wondrous scribblin's and sketchin's of his wanderin's and darin'-dos."

Lofty and Eave

She'd found this book of memoirs in his sailor's trunk, along with his clothes and the trinkets he'd brought back from overseas. She'd sorted everything out, wrapped what she couldn't use and labelled the rest.

"Myneself did be-stow it all over yonder." Eave took George's hand and dragged him over to the far wall. It was stacked to the roof with trunks, each one containing the possessions of his family, past and present, each item with a story to tell.

"Myneself will be showing you someday, yay?" said Eave.

George looked forward to seeing the sifted loft-trove left by his relatives. Knowing who they were might give him a better idea of who he was.

"I don't know anything about my family," he said rather sadly.

"Oh, yourself has a fine fambily tree," Eave smiled. George misunderstood.

"My family lived in trees?"

"Nay," she laughed. "Not like us Goffins. Not that sort of tree." She went over to the bookcase, pulled out a red leather folder and handed him a document.

"This be the Carruthers' fambily tree. Myneself did be-scribe it from clues and dockiments be-scovered in this attic."

George liked the little notes Eave had added to the tree, especially since it was she who had written in his own name. George could hardly believe what he was seeing.

"But Eave, how did you know my name before we met? How did you know I existed?"

Lofty and Eave

He was convinced there couldn't be anything in the loft with his name on it. He was born in London. He'd lived there all his life until recently. Why would anything of his be here?

But Eave had found something. It was a card which his parents had sent to Grandma Peggy and Grandpa Gordon announcing his birth.

"It did say yourself be a boy called Jowge, borned on 23 November and weighin' seven whole puddin's," recalled Eave. She'd discovered the card inside a poetry book.

Grandma Peggy must have used it as a
bookmark and at some point, Grandpa
Gordon had put the book in the attic. George
sat down on the chaise longue, put his family
tree on his knee and studied
it carefully.

"I never knew my mum's maiden name
was Derbyshire," he murmured.

He knew almost nothing about Grandma
and Grandpa Derbyshire or any of the
Derbyshires for that matter; they weren't
a close family. Did Eave know anything
about them?

"A smincey," she said, sitting down next to him. "Oh-nee this be your Pappy's fambily attic. Thus, 'tis mostly filled with Carruthers' trove. But myneself did find scribblin's which be telling of your Muppy Derbyshire."

All this talk of George's mother suddenly made him think; where was Eave's mother?

He didn't like to ask in case something terrible had happened to her, but it was almost as if Eave had read his mind.

"Whatfor be yourself pondering, Jowge?"

"Just wondering." he said. "Do you have any brothers or sisters or is there only you?"

Eave bit her lip and hid her face in her skirt. George wished he'd never asked, but after a while she emerged with slightly damp cheeks.

"Myneself has a brother, Jowge," she said wistfully. "Himself be called Arch, myne ohnee brother..."

Her voice trailed off as if she was trying to picture him in her mind.

"Where does he live?" asked George.

"With myne muppy and grandmuppy."

She told him that she, Arch, Lofty and her mother had all lived together in Grandma Peggy's loft, until one day her mother and Arch had to leave to look after Granny Cloister who had seen 103 winters and was very frail.

"Mynself does miss myne brother Arch," she sighed. "Myneself has no one to play with."

George knew exactly how she felt.

"Why can't your granny come and live here?" he asked.

"Granny Cloister be too old for travillin'," Eave said. "Herself be livin' many nights away. Us Goffins darst not be drivin' cars nor cotchin' bussins. Us must be travillin' be-foots

by dark and Granny Cloister be
havin' most gammy legs."

"Why couldn't you all
go and live with her?"
wondered George.

"Herself be livin' in a
crumblin' church belfry,"
Eave explained. "'Tis too
smincey for five Goffins.
Pappy would be forever
blammin' his head on
the bells. Thus Arch,
myne olderly brother
did go to help Muppy
and myneself did stay
to help Pappy."

"Pah!" joked Lofty.
Eave wagged
her finger at him
playfully.

"Pappy! Myneself be *most* helpful and yourself knows it."

Lofty gave her a big squeeze.

"Myneself and Littley be gettin' by just grandly on us own."

"It's a shame you can't all be together though," said George.

Eave screwed up her nose and shrugged. "Goffin fambilies be a-splittin' oftentimes, Jowge. Roof space be sorrofill rare, but merrilee us be to-gathered in yondertimes, Muppy did say."

"What's your mum's name?" asked George.

"Herself be called Ariel," said Eave.

"Ariel? That's nice," he said. "Mine's called Susan."

Eave wagged her finger at him.

"Nay, Jowge. Not Susan. 'Tis Susykins!"

It turned out that Eave had read the love letters his mother had sent to his father. She'd found them in the back of an old wallet.

"Herself did write, 'To my darling Phillip with love from Susykins—'"

George cut her short.

"Yes, all right ... ugh." He shuddered.

The idea of his parents being madly in love and calling each other soppy names made him feel queasy.

"Mynself will be showin' you these heartfelt scribblin's soontimes!" laughed Eave.

Just then, Lofty appeared and patted her on the shoulder.

"Betterly be showin' Jowge now," he said solemnly.

"Tomorrow us be movin' on."

Eave's eyes filled with tears
again. George's heart sank.

"Why?" he asked.
"Why do you have
to go tomorrow?"

Lofty picked up
an empty suitcase and
started to pack.

"When somebiddy be movin' in Down
Below, us Goffins must be movin' out."

"But Grandma Peggy's always lived here
and you didn't leave," George protested. "She
must have heard you in the loft."

Lofty and Eave exchanged glances.

"Nay," said Lofty, "Us be livin' a-loft for
many summers with no miseree. Her Below
be terrible hard of hearin'. But now us has
been heard."

"Jowge's Pappy has most normous ears,"
grumbled Eave.

She stretched her own tiny ears sideways
– George couldn't help smiling.

"Whyfor be you larfin at myneself?" she pouted.

But he wasn't laughing at her. He was smiling because he was happy. He'd thought he would be lonely all summer but now he'd found someone to talk to. Someone far more interesting than anyone he'd ever known, right under his roof.

"Don't go," he said. "I won't tell anyone you're here, I promise. I'll protect you."

Lofty took Eave aside and mumbled behind his hand.

"Hmm ... but howfor can us be trustin' Jowge, Littley?"

They paced up and down in unison looking very thoughtful, then Eave took Lofty aside, unfolded his left ear from inside

his helmet and whispered something. Lofty listened intently, then he rubbed his stomach and whispered back to Eave.

"Yay!" exclaimed Eave.

She took hold of George's hands and whirled him round on the bearskin rug.

"Pappy did say if yourself be-fetches the jam biskies, us will be most trustin."

George was dizzy from being spun, so Eave propped him up against the bookcase until the room stopped spinning.

"I won't let you down," he said. "I'll get the biscuits off Grandma first thing tomorrow."

Eave and Lofty shook their heads in unison.

"Nay, Jowge. Be-fetch the biskies now!"

CHAPTER FOUR

CHIMBLEY EGGS

It was almost dawn, but George knew he had to set off on his mission. He was struggling to stay awake but he had to rescue the biscuits from Grandma's room without waking her and bring them up to Lofty and Eave.

He crept down the top flight of stairs but they were so creaky, he had to straddle the bannisters and slide down to the ground floor. As he stood outside Grandma Peggy's door, he thought of all the things that could go wrong; maybe his mum had already taken the biscuits away. Maybe Grandma had eaten them after all.

Lofty and Eave

She was snoring,
so George padded into
her room and began
his search. There
wasn't a crumb to be
found. The biscuits had
gone. Now what?

He was just
wondering if he should
raid the biscuit tin in
the kitchen when he
heard a clatter out in
the garden. Was there
a burglar?

George peered
behind the curtain in
disbelief. Somebody
was trying to steal
something. There was
a bird table outside.
On it was the basket of
biscuits. Above the basket,

he could see a length of fishing
line with a big hook tied to the end.
The hook swung back and forth. As
soon as it caught the basket handle,
the line was reeled back in and the
biscuits rose up into the sky.

George tried to unlock the French
doors as quietly as he could so that
he could go out and investigate
but the key was stiff and when he
turned it, it gave a sharp click.

"What are you doing, boy?"

He almost jumped out of his
skin. He'd woken Grandma Peggy.
Lofty had said that Grandma was
hard of hearing but now George
wasn't so sure.

"I – burglars!" he said.

"Eh?"

He raised his voice as loudly as he
dared without waking his parents.

"I thought it was burglars."

"I never heard anything," she said. "Leave the curtains alone, boy."

She seemed agitated, as if there was something out there she didn't want him to see. An interesting thought crossed George's mind. Why hadn't Grandma just put the biscuits on the bird table? Why put the basket out too? And why did she have biscuits brought to her in a basket with a handle instead of on a plate?

Maybe she knew about the Goffins! Maybe she was feeding them secretly and left the basket on the bird table every night, loaded with provisions for them to hook up to the loft. He daren't ask her outright – he'd promised Lofty and Eave

he'd never tell anyone they existed – so he tried to trick her into telling him.

"Grandma, why did you put the basket out for the birds and not just the biscuits?"

"Basket? Did I? I wondered where it had gone." She grabbed his arm. "Here, don't tell anyone, boy. They'll put me in a home. I don't want to go in one of those. They're full of old people."

George wasn't sure if Grandma was being daft or devious, but he knew what he'd just seen and he was pretty sure where the biscuits had gone. He crept back to his room and knocked softly on the green door.

He'd agreed to use the same knock every time so that the Goffins would know it was him: one long knock followed by four short ones and two quick ones.

Pom ... tiddy pom pom ... pom pom!

Eave answered it. She'd tied her hair into messy plaits which bounced like copper springs whenever she moved.

"Jowge! Wherefor has yourself been? Has you hooked us biskies and swollied them?"

She had jam all round her mouth.

"Whyfor be you grinnin' at myneself, Jowge?"

"Crumbs, Eave." He flicked one off her chin. Eave blushed, wafted herself with a Chinese fan and stepped aside as George went into the loft. By now, the dawn sun was streaming in through the skylight.

"I saw a fishing line, Eave," he said. "Someone hooked Grandma's basket up."

"'Twas myneself!" called Lofty. "Oftentimes us does roof-fish from the sky-like. Sometimes us does fish for veggibles, sometimes

fruitibles. Sometimes us does cast the line
to yonder lawn and fish for bird-bread, but
tonight myneself did cotch a haul of biskies."

His voice was coming from behind a
curtain made from a row of plastic macs.
George whipped it back. Lofty was sitting
naked in a tin bath washing his armpits with
a bar of strong-smelling, yellow soap. George
went scarlet, so Eave fanned him vigorously.

75

"Great-Great-Grandmuppy Maud's fan be a goodly cure for blushin's, Jowge!"

She smiled and then offered to show him round the attic so he could see how they lived.

"This be where us does bathe," she said, "unless it be a-drizzlin', then us does shower nakey on the roof. Oh and Jowge – this be where myneself does wash myne face."

She pointed to a Victorian washstand which held a chipped china bowl painted with pansies.

"Really? Where's your loo?" asked George.

He'd been wondering about that for sometime. Eave looked at him quizzically.

"Myne ... loo?"

"The toilet," he explained. "Where do you ... you know?"

He did the actions and, finally, the penny dropped.

"Ah!" said Eave. "Yourself be wishin' to use myne closet, yay?"

She led him to a tall cupboard and flung open the door. The shelves had all been removed except for the middle one, which had a large hole cut in it. Below the hole was a tin bucket which stood on a pile of towels – probably to muffle any sound effects. She patted the shelf.

"Be myne guest, Jowge!"

She ushered him into the cubicle.

"I'm fine," he said. "I don't need to go. I went earlier."

"Sit, Jowge!" she insisted. "'Tis most comftible."

He sat down on the makeshift seat with his trousers on, just to keep her quiet. He noticed that a fierce-looking hook had been screwed into the wood at waist height to hold the toilet paper.

"Great-Great-Grandpappy Montague did grapple that deadly hook from a motley pirate who did foolishly scupper his whalin' ship," said Eave.

"How do you know?" asked George.

"'Tis be-scribed in his almanac in all its goryness!"

Now, instead of a cutlass, the pirate's hook held a bundle of paper napkins decorated with pictures of a very young Queen Elizabeth on her coronation day.

"Mostly us does wype with newspapey," Eave whispered behind her hand. "But myneself did put out the royal stuff for you, Jowge."

"Next time I come, I'll bring some proper toilet roll," he said. "We use the quilted sort."

Eave clapped her hands silently, so as not to awaken Them Below.

"Hark, Pappy! Jowge be fetchin' us quilted," said Eave. "Think how plush!"

As George stood up, he accidentally kicked the bucket and it fell over. It didn't make a noise because of the towels and luckily there was nothing in it, but it made him wonder... He had to ask.

"Where do you empty it? Do you just chuck it out of the skylight?"

Lofty and Eave

Lofty re-appeared in a green silk smoking jacket. It must have once belonged to someone much taller than him. It billowed round his calves and although it made a lousy jacket, it made an excellent Goffin dressing gown. He bent down and picked up the bucket.

"Chuck it out?" he exclaimed. "Nay! There be a soil pipe on the outer wall. Myneself does clamber onto yonder roof and pour it pipewards into the drain."

"What if someone sees you?" asked George.

Lofty smiled at him as if he was a bit simple.

"'Tis rare for your kind to be lookin' up," he said.

"And 'tis even rarer for us kind not to be lookin' down," added Eave.

Her top lip was still smeared with jam. There was a mirror on the wall above the washstand but it was too high for her to see into properly.

"You haven't washed your face yet, have you?" said George.

"Myneself has!"

He lifted her up by the waist so she could see her reflection. She hardly weighed a thing. She was too thin, George thought.

"'Tis most stubborn jam," Eave declared, wiping her mouth on her sleeve. "Myneself hasn't tasted jam for so a-long."

"How do you survive?" asked George. From what Eave had told him, he guessed they couldn't go shopping in the high street. "Are there special Goffin shops? What do you do for money?"

The Goffins

Eave threw back her head and laughed.

"Shops? Goffins doesn't do shops and munnee, Jowge."

"But where do you get food and drink? Does Grandma leave it out for you?"

She shook her head so hard, her plaits whipped his face.

"Nay! Herself does oh-nee feed the birds. Us does roof-fish for milk and loaves but mostly us does feast at nature's table. Does yourself be hungry, Jowge? Myneself could be cookin' you a chimbley egg."

"Eggs? Where do you get eggs?"

Eave led him to a ladder propped against the skylight and climbed to the top.

"Come, Jowge. Come see wherefor be the eggs."

He climbed
after her. He could
hear a crooning
noise above his
head. There was
a pigeon asleep
in a pie dish under
the rafters.

"Herself be called
Chimbley," said Eave.
She slipped her hand
under the pigeon and
removed a small warm egg
which she placed in George's
palm.

"Breakfeast!" she announced.
"Shall myneself be frizzlin' or
broilin' it, Jowge?"

"You can cook?"

"Yay," said Eave, as if it was the dumbest question in the world. George, who had never cooked anything in his life, said he'd like his chimbley egg boiled. She reached out and produced a jug.

"Us best be-fetchin' some water then, Jowge."

There was a big tank in the loft mounted on the ceiling joists which supplied the whole house with water through various pipes. It was constantly refilling so no one Down Below would notice if a Goffin used a few gallons to fill a bath or do the washing.

"But us must be-fetch rain and leaf-sweat from yonder garden for drinkin' and cookin'!" said Eave.

George was surprised. "You fetch water from Grandma Peggy's garden?"

Grandma might be deaf but she wasn't blind.

"Nay!" Eave laughed. "From us roof garden. 'Tis a wonder to behold."

"There's a roof garden?"

"Every Goffin does have a roof garden. 'Tis that or starve." Eave pushed the skylight open. "Come see, Jowge!"

CHAPTER FIVE

ROOFUS

George climbed out on to the roof. His legs were shaking. He didn't have a great head for heights and he was scared he would slip. Eave took his hand to steady him.

"Yourself be sky-dizzy, that's all."

She told him he'd get his roof legs in no time, but George wasn't convinced. He sat down, pressed his back against the wall and clung to the skylight sill with one hand. When his stomach finally stopped lurching, he began to admire the garden Eave had created up in the clouds. It was only small, but every surface had been put to good use.

Cherry tomatoes tumbled from the chimney pots. All around the stack, Eave had hung kettles, pans, baskets, straw hats, riding boots and even an old army helmet to grow things in. She tapped the helmet with her finger and it swung gently on its strap.

"Your Great-Grandpappy Sid did wear that lid in Worldly War One, Jowge," she said.

"How d'you know?" he asked. "Did you find photos of him?"

"Myneself did be-scover more than that, Jowge." She'd discovered the letters that Sid had sent from the trenches to his family.

"They be
in a box with
his medals, all roly-
round with ribbon," she said.

"He won medals?"

"Yay, Jowge. Great-Grandpappy Sid be
lionbrave. Himself did boldly charge through
cannon fire on his trusty mule and thus did
rescue many a fallen soldier."

She'd filled the helmet with poppies.
George watched them nodding in the breeze
and in that moment, the First World War
became personal. It wasn't just a load of
battles he had to remember dates for at
school; his great-grandfather had fought there.

Lofty and Eave

His own flesh and blood had helped to defeat the enemy. If George hadn't met Eave, he'd never have known that, because he never bothered to listen when his dad tried to tell him about the past. What other amazing stories must he have missed?

"Jowge, whatfor be yourself a-thinkin'?" whispered Eave.

"Great-Grandpa – was he killed?" he asked, wincing at the bullet hole in the helmet which now served as a drainage hole for the plants.

"Nay", said Eave. "Himself did lose a leg at the Battle of Somme but all was not lost." She grabbed hold of one foot and hopped up and down on the roof playfully.

"Soldier Sidney did journey home and himself did betrothe his darlin' Dolly."

"So they got married and she became my ... Great-Grandma Dolly?"

"Yay!" Eave lowered her voice, "Myneself be wearing her knickybockers, Jowge."

The hanging containers overflowed with vegetables, fruit and flowers planted in a mixture of mud and leaves scraped from the gutter. The biggest plants had plastic bags tied around them which were wet with condensation. Eave moved fearlessly across the roof, undoing each bag in turn and letting the water droplets trickle into her jug.

There wasn't
enough to cook a wren's
egg, let alone a pigeon's, so she topped it up
with rain water. It had collected in a pool at
the bottom of a hammock strung between the
aerial and the weathercock.

"I bet that's dad's old hammock," groaned
George. "He's always going on about when
he was a boy scout and how I should join, but
scouts is stupid."

Secretly, George had always wanted to be a scout, but because his friends didn't go, he didn't go either, in case they called him a wuss behind his back.

As it turned out, the hammock didn't belong to his father at all, it was Great-Great-Grandpa Monty's. According to his almanac, which Eave claimed to have read from cover to cover, he'd slept in it slung between two trees in the deepest, darkest African Jungle.

"Himself be almost gargled by a serpent, Jowge!" she exclaimed.

The almanac didn't go into detail about how he escaped suffocation by the snake, but noted that if it hadn't been for the quick-thinking of his loyal guide, Bubba Tundi, he'd have been a dead man.

"Yourself be lookin' just like him, Jowge."

"Who, Bubba Tundi?"

"Nay," she laughed. "Like Great-Great-Grandpappy Montague."

Lofty and Eave

Eave plucked a strawberry from the plant and balanced it on George's knee. He picked it up in his teeth and tried to make it look as if he'd done it for a laugh, but actually he was still afraid to let go of the ledge. He wished he'd inherited his great-great-grandfather's courage instead of his looks. Just then, he made the mistake of looking down and shivered.

"'Tis betterly not to be peekin' Down Below 'til yourself be sky-savvy," said Eave.

George hastily changed the subject to take his mind off plummeting to his death.

"Where did you get the strawberry plants from, Eave? Come to that, where did you get any of these plants?"

"The westerly wind does blow seeds into the roof moss," she said. "Myneself be growin' dandyloons for salad and chickeree for coffee and all."

"But the wind can't blow tomato pips," said George. "Where did your tomatoes come from?"

"Doesn't yourself be knowin' nothin'?" asked Eave with a grin. "Chimbley does pass pips and pods in pigeon doin's, ripe for plantin' ... apples, goobies, tomatoes, all sorts." She pointed to a small tree which she'd trained along wires fixed to the brickwork. "Per-lum," she said. "Myneself be growin' it from a stone."

George winced. How could a pigeon pass something as big as a plum stone?

"Nay," Eave giggled. "Myne perlum stone be a gift from Roofus," giggled Eave.

"Who's Roofus?"

She sprang like a mountain goat to the edge of the roof, leant right over and clicked her tongue.

"Tch-tch-tch."

95

Lofty and Eave

George wanted to yell, "Be careful!" but he didn't dare in case he startled her and she fell. He needn't have worried. Eave seemed oblivious to the danger.

"Mynself be borned on a roof!" she sang.

Even so, Lofty had added a few safety features which she pointed out to him.

"See how Pappy did be-fix that horse-sittle over yonder?"

Sure enough, there was a leather saddle attached to the pointy part of the roof, right at the front. No doubt it used to belong to Great-Great-Uncle Cecil's stallion but now the Goffins were using it as a fishing stool.

"Will yourself be learning to roof-ride, Jowge?" asked Eave.

"Maybe not today."

"Shame!" she said. "'Tis normous fun!"

To his horror, she jumped into the saddle, stood up in the stirrups and pretended to cast a fishing line into next door's garden.

"Please get down," he whispered. "Please, please get down. It's so dangerous."

But Eave was as happy in that saddle forty feet up in the air as a kid on a donkey at the seaside. Finally, she dismounted and he could breathe again.

"Has yourself ever been fishin', Jowge?"

"Once," he said. "But only for tadpoles."

"With your Pappy, yay?"

George looked away. His dad had been busy that day. In fact, he seemed to be busy every day these days. They hadn't done anything together for a long time – nothing fun anyway. Suddenly it seemed to matter.

"I've never been fishing with him, Eave."

"Not never? Doesn't yourself be sad, Jowge?"

"I'm kind of used to it." He shrugged. "He does his dad things and I just..."

George trailed off. He'd got used to doing his own thing, but after seeing how close Eave and Lofty were, he wondered if he was missing out.

"Maybe 'tis how fambilies Down Below does carry on, Jowge," she mused. "'Tis not the Goffin way."

There was a washing line strung between

two chimneys which she hung onto as casually
as if she was riding a tube train. Some clothes
had been pegged out, including a pair of frilly
drawers. They looked positively Victorian and
George was just joking to himself that they
might be his Great-Great-Uncle Cecil's when
Eave caught him looking at them.

"Yourself darst not be peekin' at myne
bloomin's, Jowge!" she scolded.

"I wasn't!"

"Myneself did cotch you!"

99

She thought it was so funny, she did a little dance and swished her skirt about. George could barely look. He was certain she'd slip over the edge.

"Please hold onto the washing line, Eave!"

She flapped her hands at him.

"Oh, Jowge."

She sat down next to him, rolling her eyes.

"Yourself be worse than myne Muppy."

"Do you miss her?" he blurted.

For a moment, Eave looked tearful. "Yay, myneself does miss Muppy most terrible. And Arch."

"I miss my friends too," admitted George.

He told her about Warren, Dino and Jermaine and how angry he was that he'd had to come and live with Grandma Peggy who didn't even seem to like him. He'd been made to leave his old house, his old school, his old life – it just wasn't fair!

"It wouldn't be so bad if I had a brother or sister to talk to," he sighed. "But I never will."

Eave rested her head on his shoulder.

"Myneself will be your step-in sister, Jowge. Yourself can be myne step-in brother and then us won't be a-loney any more, yay?"

George liked the idea of having a sister, but was it sissy? He thought about it for a minute and decided he didn't care. Jermaine and Dino weren't around to tease him and although Warren's sister was a pain, she wasn't a Goffin. She wasn't like Eave.

"Yay!" he grinned.

"And Jowge? Myneself be yearnin' for you to befriend Grandmuppy Peg. 'Tis a must to be knowin' herself or howfor will yourself ever be knowin' himself?"

George was scrabbling around to find something equally deep and meaningful to say when Eave put her finger to her lips.

"Shhh."

"Why? Is someone Down Below?"

She pointed to the side of the roof.

"Hark! Roofus cometh."

A grey squirrel popped its head above the gutter and swivelled its ears.

"Come, Roofus!" called Eave. "Come say halloo to Jowge."

The squirrel ran towards her, but when George moved his foot, it stopped in its tracks. Eave clicked her fingers.

"Whyfor be yourself shy, Roofus? 'Tis oh-nee myne step-in brother. Himself be peacefun. Jowge, be givin' Roofus a strawberry."

He really didn't want to let go of the ledge so Eave reached inside the skylight, winched up an anchor and hooked it under a beam. It was a serious piece of hardware.

"Woah, where'd you get that?" asked George.

"It did be-fall off a whalin' ship – or so it does say in Great-Great-Grandpa Monty's almanac."

Originally the anchor had been on a heavy

chain, but the chain was too noisy for a Goffin to use without giving away his whereabouts, so Lofty had replaced it with rope. Eave handed the end to George.

"I'm not scared exactly," he said.

"Nor be yourself a Goffin exactly," she said. "Hold fast."

George held on and leaned forward to offer a strawberry to the squirrel. Roofus sat and washed his whiskers, looking at George, then the strawberry, then George again.

"Take it!" he begged.

Hurry up and take it, he thought. *In case this anchor slips and I let go of the rope.*

"Oooh ... Roofus be bringin' us a gift," said Eave. "Spit, Roofus!"

She'd trained him to bring her all sorts of things from the garden. Depending on the season, he'd bring fruit, nuts and berries. Once, he even brought some olives.

Today he had cherries which he spat out of his cheek pouches into George's lap. Then he gobbled up the strawberry and scampered off.

"Good Squill!" Eave called after him. She chewed the flesh off the ripest cherry and cleaned the stone on her skirt.

"Now myneself can be growin' cheeries. If oh-nee us did have some flour, myneself could be bakin' you a cheery pie!"

George added flour to his mental list of things to fetch. Then he remembered he'd seen a packet of frozen pastry in the downstairs freezer. Eave had never heard of frozen pastry and was so excited by the idea, he promised to bring her some.

"How will you bake the pie though?" he asked. "Where's your oven?"

"Us has two; one outwards and one inwards, Jowge. Goffins be most happy cookin' in the clouds, but us must oh-nee do it when the wind be blowin' rightly or smoke be risin' from the chimbley. Otherwise, Them

Below will be sniffin' the cookin' whiffs from Above."

There was a flat roof below the main roof which could be reached by climbing down a series of croquet hoops that had been hammered into the brickwork – "Pappy did blam them in whilst it be a-thundering!" – and at the bottom of these stairs was a small cast-iron stove on the flat roof. It looked an awfully long way down. George didn't fancy risking his neck just to boil a Chimbley egg so he was very relieved when Eave suggested cooking it indoors.

She was just about to help him back into the attic when they heard a van pull up Down Below. Someone got out, a dog barked, then the doorbell rang. Eave turned deathly pale.

It was her turn to be scared.

Chapter Six

ALMOST COTCHED

It was the rat catcher. He had a loud voice which carried over the rooftop from the front garden. George could hear him talking to his father on the doorstep.

"Problem in the loft?" he said. "Don't you worry, guv. This dog's the best ratter in the county. He'll soon flush the beggars out. Come on, Satan. In we go, son."

"Hastily, Jowge!" gasped Eave, shoving him back through the skylight in her hurry to alert her father.

"Fi! 'Tis the rat catcher, Pappy! Them Below is comin' up! Whatever shall us do?"

"Trash and hide!" he panicked. "Trash and hide!"

George watched dumbstruck as they tried desperately – silently – to shift the furniture and bric-a-brac to make the loft look less like rooms

and more like junk. They turned paintings to the wall, pulled up the bearskin rug and

threw old curtains and sheets over anything too heavy to move. Finally, they put Chimbley out with the pie dish and disappeared.

"Where are you?" whispered George. "You can't hide here. Even if the rat catcher can't see you, his dog will sniff you out!"

Lofty and Eave reappeared as mysteriously as they'd vanished.

"'Tis the truth," sighed Lofty. "A hound be whiffin' the faintest sniff."

"But yourself did bathe, Pappy. Mynself did scrub myne face!" sobbed Eave. "See?"

She stuck out her jam-free chin miserably for George to inspect.

"There's only one thing for it," he said. "You'll have to hide in my bedroom."

It was risky, but he'd promised to protect them and he couldn't think of a better way. He could hear the rat catcher talking to his father in the kitchen. There wasn't a moment to lose. He opened the green door and pushed Eave through.

"Ooh!" she said. "'Tis a goodly chamber. Whatfor does this do?"

She'd picked up his mobile phone. George grabbed it.

"Don't press anything, Eave. Get under my bed and don't say a word!"

"George?" called his dad.

George opened his wardrobe and tried to squeeze Lofty in amongst the countless clothes and toys and shoes. He wouldn't fit.

"Lose the helmet, Lofty. Quick, give me that harpoon."

His father was coming up the stairs. George managed to wrap the horseguards helmet in his dressing gown but where could he hide the harpoon? It wasn't a small thing and he was afraid that if he shoved it under the bed, he'd poke Eave and she'd scream and give the game away.

Thinking rapidly, he threaded it through his old school belt and hung it out of the slanted window. He prayed the belt was strong enough to hold it and that no one down below would look up and see it.

"George?"

"Dad."

George snapped his TV on and pretended to be watching it.

"This is Mr Stow," said his father. "He needs to come through and check the loft."

"All right, mate?" said the rat catcher.

George looked the man up and down.

"Where's your dog?" he asked.

George's father groaned. "As soon as your Grandma got wind of Mr Stow's terrier, she refused to let him use it," he explained. "She thinks it's squirrels, not rats. Kept going on about dogs murdering helpless fluffy animals in her own home. We thought it best not to upset her, so we've left the dog in her room."

Lofty and Eave

A girlish giggle escaped from under the bed. George coughed to try and cover it up.

"It's not funny," said his father. "You won't be laughing if you find a rat under your bed."

"Oh?" said Mr Stow. "Have you seen droppings under there, lad?"

He bent down to have a look.

"Don't!" said George. "Don't look, it's horrible. Old socks ... pizzas."

His father looked faintly embarrassed.

"Kids, eh?" he said.

"Got one just like him," said Mr Stow.

He straightened up and waved his rat trap amiably at George.

"All right if I go through, mate?"

"I could put the trap in the loft," said George. "I've always wanted to be a rat catcher."

Mr Stow looked most offended.

"The catching of rats is a specialist skill," he said. "You can't just bung the trap down any old how. There's a knack to it."

"Let the man get on with his job, George," insisted his dad.

Mr Stow opened the green door and went into the loft. George's father tutted loudly at the TV.

"You'll go blind watching that thing all day, George. Go and kick a ball about."

"Got no one to play with, Dad. Unless you want to go in goal?"

His dad looked at him for a second, then chuntered something about being too busy and set off back downstairs leaving George alone in the room – only he wasn't quite alone.

"Jowge!"

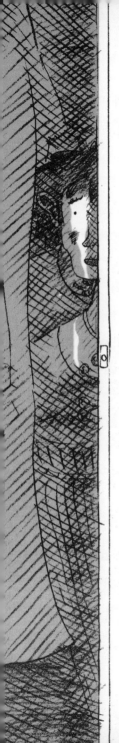

Lofty and Eave

Lofty opened the wardrobe a crack.

"What is it, Lofty? Can't you breathe?"

George wafted the door for a moment so that the air could circulate.

"Jowge, myneself did never empty the bath!" confessed Lofty.

There would be wet soap, a damp towel – evidence that someone (and certainly not a dirty rat) was living in the attic.

"I'll cause a diversion," said George. "Stay there, Lofty. Don't speak. Don't move."

"Myneself has leg-crampy, Jowge," bleated Eave.

He felt under the bed and patted his little step-in sister on the head.

"Shush! Be lionbrave. Like Great-Grandpa Sid, OK?"

"Yay."

George ran downstairs and headed straight for Grandma's room. Mr Stow's terrier was sitting on her bed chewing her cardigan.

"Grandma," said George, "there's someone in your loft."

Grandma gazed at the ceiling.

"There never is, boy. It's just your imagination."

"No it isn't, it's the rat catcher," he said.

Grandma sat up straight and George thought he detected a flicker of panic.

"I'm not having that man trapping squirrels," she said. "I stopped him taking his dog up, see?"

"Grandma, I think we should do something. I'm very fond of ... squirrels. I mean, there might be a family of them."

"There might," said Grandma. "I wouldn't want them to come to any harm, boy."

Then without warning, she did the most awful thing. She took her false teeth out, clacked them at the dog and threw them in the air. The terrier leapt up, caught them in his mouth and ran off.

"Dogth got my teef, boy. Call the rat man!" she whooped.

George ran up the stairs faster than he'd ever run in his life. He burst into his bedroom and banged on the green door, yelling as loudly as he could and not a moment too soon; the rat catcher had just spotted a pigeon's egg in the loft. Nothing unusual about that, except that it was sitting on a silver spoon next to a copper pan, looking for all the world as if it was about to be boiled but the cook had left in a hurry.

"Mr Stow? Come quick!" shouted George. "Satan's stolen Grandma's teeth!"

The rat catcher blundered out of the loft with his glasses askew.

"He never? Oh, my days! SATAN! C'mere!"

He ran after the dog which seemed to be thoroughly enjoying the game, romping from room to room with a red-faced Mr Stow cursing and wheezing behind him.

Finally, having peed against the umbrella stand, Satan was cornered in the kitchen where he sat baring Grandma's dentures and refusing to give them back until George's mother gave him a sausage. Mr Stow was deeply apologetic.

"His bark's worse than his bite," he reassured them. "The good news is, I can't see no sign of rats. Most likely a pigeon come in through a hole in the roof, then flew out."

The bad news was that Grandma would have to get some new dentures. The old ones were so badly chewed they looked as if they belonged to a werewolf. When George showed them to her, she threw back her head and laughed.

"Here, my barksh worsh than my bite, boy! A-ha-ha-haaaaa!"

She winked at him, offered him a toffee and showed him her gums.

"Be a pal. Shew that for me, lad!" she chortled.

They were sharing a joke and in that moment, George felt himself warming to Grandma enormously.

CHAPTER SEVEN

HONEY AND KINDNESS

After the rat catcher had left, George's parents went into town to buy groceries and to order a new set of teeth for Grandma Peggy, who was having to make do with her spare set.

"Keep her company, George," said Dad.

For once, he'd have been happy to – they'd had such a laugh – but Grandma had gone to sleep. And as his parents were out, he was able to release Lofty and Eave from their hiding places in his bedroom without fear of discovery.

They seemed in no hurry to go back to the loft though. Eave was fascinated by his television. She'd never seen one before – not plugged in anyway.

"Howfor does the peepil be fittin' inside, Jowge?"

He tried to explain but he didn't really understand the technology himself. He let her watch it for a few minutes, promising that one day, when everyone was out, she could watch it again. Meanwhile, Lofty had found George's

old Game Boy and was holding it to his ear
and dancing.

"It's not a radio, Lofty," George laughed.
"It's a game. Press that button ... see?"

Lofty's eyes almost popped out of his head.
He sat down on George's bed, mesmerized by
the strange, bright creatures moving across
the miniature screen.

"Whatfor does these beasts be called?" he
breathed.

"Pokemon," said George. "They're not real

– they're like cartoons? That one's called Pikachu and that one's called – oh, who cares? It's a very old game."

Not surprisingly, Lofty didn't have a clue what he was talking about. As for being old, the toy was much newer than anything Lofty had ever come across. He didn't want to put it down.

"You have to go back in the loft *now*," said George.

"Nay. Myneself does like it here," protested Eave.

She'd found his Rollerblades. Before he could stop her, she'd slipped them on and tried to stand up in them.

They were much too big for her and her ankles went. She flailed her arms and George dashed forward and caught her.

"Yourself has most funny boots, Jowge!" she laughed.

"Come on," he said. "It'll take ages to put your rooms straight after you trashed them. If we do it while Mum and Dad are out, it won't matter if we make a noise."

Lofty pretended not to be listening.

"If you come now, I'll let you borrow my Game Boy," said George. "Here's your helmet."

He switched the TV off and packed a small bag with bits and pieces he thought the Goffins might enjoy: some bubble gum, some felt-tips, half a packet of mints. They were thrilled.

"Best not be forgettin' myne deadly 'poon," said Lofty.

He hauled the harpoon back inside and they all went back into the attic. While George helped Lofty shift the furniture, Eave went

off to prepare the breakfast that had been so
rudely interrupted by the rat catcher.

"Does yourself be likin'
honnee, Jowge?" she called.
It was then that
George noticed a low
buzzing sound. There
was a bees' nest in
the loft. Eave stopped
what she was doing and
showed him the little hole
in the wall where they flew
in and out. The swarm had arrived
last June and set up home in a
cavity under the roof. Here
they raised baby bees
and built honeycombs.

"Pappy does gather
the honnee and wax,
Jowge," said Eave.

"Doesn't he get
stung?"

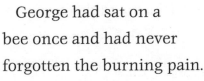

George had sat on a
bee once and had never
forgotten the burning pain.

"Nay! Us Goffins be bee-
savvy," said Eave. They'd kept
bees for generations and they
knew how to avoid annoying them.

"A bee-stung Goffin
be rarer than buttyfly
teeth," she announced.
"Myneself does roll the
beeswax into candils
... come see."

She led him into
a room
which was
furnished

with a pair of bedside cabinets,
a carpenter's bench,
a wardrobe with a round
window and various crates,
boxes and hampers.

127

These had been arranged
to form an L-shaped kitchen,
complete with various work
surfaces and storage space.
Along with the boxes of
knobbly hand made candles,
there were all sorts of
fascinating items on display,
including a life-sized figurine
of an Indian boy holding a
tray, an alarming collection of
sabres, daggers and penknives
and a stuffed cockerel.

"And this be myne cooking
hat," said Eave, placing a fluted
copper bowl on her head.

"That's a jelly mould," said
George.

The gaps between the floor
rafters had been packed with
old blankets to muffle the
sound of Goffin footsteps.

Lofty and Eave

Over this, Lofty had laid a roll of leftover
lino. George recognized the pattern at once:
Grandma Peggy still had it in her kitchen
downstairs. It looked as though it had never
been replaced – George's father had
probably learnt to walk on it.

Eave's kitchen had no gas, electricity
or running water, but there was a
wash tub which doubled as a
sink and an iron gadget on
legs with a roller and a
handle. It looked like an
instrument of torture
but George knew it was
a mangle – he'd seen
one in a museum on a
school trip. Jermaine
had fed Warren's
tie between
the rollers and
almost strangled
him.

"'Tis a wringle, Jowge," insisted Eave. "Mynself does use it to wring the washin' – just like Violet."

"Who's Violet?" asked George.

"Herself be your Great-Great-Grandmuppy Maud's maid in yestertimes."

Violet must have slept in my bedroom, thought George. His mum had told him it used to be the servant's room. It was weird to think Violet had trodden on the same floorboards and looked at the same moon out of the same window.

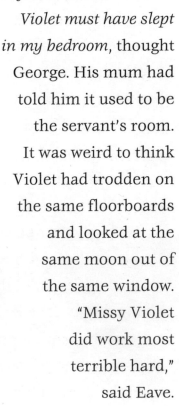

"Missy Violet did work most terrible hard," said Eave.

131

Great-Great-Grandma Maud had six children. Their names were all written down on the Carruthers family tree: Cecil, Agnes, Percy, Florence, Sid and Victoria. That was an awful lot of dirty clothes.

"My mum has a washing machine," said George. "It washes the clothes automatically."

He looked at Eave's hands and saw that they were red and rough. He thought about sneaking some of her laundry into his linen basket so that his mum could wash it, but how would he explain the sudden appearance of girls' clothing?

"I'll take it to the launderette for you," he said. "But it costs a lot of money."

He'd only ever been in a launderette once. He ran in there with Dino after a game of football to get out of the rain. It had been fun sitting there in the warm, sharing a kebab and watching other people's pants and socks going round in the soapy water. He knew how to work the machines – he'd watched an old

lady do it – but she had to use a lot of coins.
It was all very expensive.

"Munnee be most expensive, Jowge," said
Eave. "Goffins doesn't be needin' munnee.
Us be swappin' things or us does pay with a
Kindness. Or us does a Kindness for free."

George couldn't remember the last time
he'd done a Kindness for free. He never tidied
his room or offered to do chores around
the house. His mum nagged him to but she
always ended up doing it herself. He'd felt
quite smug about it, but when he told Eave,
she was shocked.

"Fi! Yourself be never cleanin' nor cookin'?"

"That's my mum's job," he wheedled.

Eave blinked at him in disbelief.

"But yourself be helpin' your Pappy with
the fixin' and the diggin', yay?"

"Erm..." George had never helped his dad
either. He never offered to wash the car or
weed the garden or anything.

"Oh, Jowge," sighed Eave. "For shame!

Yourself be ten summers old! Myne brother
Arch be oh-nee twelve summers yet himself
be choppin', cookin' and fishin' like a
genteelman."

George hung his head. He felt pathetic and
lazy. He wanted Eave to be proud of him.
He wanted to be a good step-in brother, so
he tried to think of a Kindness he could do.
Despite having never boiled an egg before,
he offered to help her with breakfast.

"Where's the oven?" he asked.

She fetched a small, iron box and put it on
the table.

"This be Great-Great-Grandpappy
Montague's old camping stove."

She unfolded the legs and opened it out
to reveal a compartment for burning fuel.
It also had a metal grill and a flat griddle
just big enough to hold a small kettle, a pan
or a pot. It had been halfway round the
world, this stove. It had boiled snake's
eggs. It had grilled crocodile steaks.

"It even be cookin' a cassowilly casserole!"
Eave declared.

"Cassowilly?" exclaimed George. "Are you
sure?"

"Yay! Montague did scribe howfor to be
roastin' a cassowilly."

Seeing that he didn't believe her, Eave
insisted on fetching the almanac. She
disappeared for a few moments, then
returned with a large book, bound in scuffed
leather. She had balanced it on a velvet
cushion and was wearing a pair of peach
silk gloves which went up to her
armpits and were rather too
long in the fingers.

"'Tis most delicate," she told
him. "Does yourself be
havin' clean hands,
Jowge?"

He held them out for inspection and once Eave was satisfied they were clean, she began flicking through the almanac for the recipe pages.

"Wherefor be that cassowilly...?"

George was dying to grab the book and look at it properly. As he glanced over Eave's shoulder, he kept getting tantalizing glimpses of the contents: hand-drawn maps, sketches of animals, foreign stamps, diary entries, all sorts.

"Ho!" said Eave, tapping one of the pages. "See Jowge? Cassowilly casserole."

"You mean Cassowary!"

He'd heard of one of those; it was an Australian bird.

"Yay," said Eave, "Cassowilly. That be what mynself did say. Great-Great-Grandpappy Montague did feast on goodly fare no matter where himself a-wandered."

"Thus himself did have heroic strength to defeat ferocious beasts," said Lofty.

"And vile lurgies," added Eave. "Whatfor does yourself be feastin' on mostly, Jowge?"

"Burgers, chips and pizza." He knew they weren't good for him but he liked them because he didn't have to chew much. To be honest, he did feel a bit flabby and unfit.

"Veggibles, fruitibles and fine meat," said Lofty. "'Tis the stuff of heroes."

George vowed to change his diet. If he wanted to be fit enough to wrestle pythons like his Great-Great-Grandpa, he must start eating properly.

Eave poured some water from her jug into a copper pan and lowered the Chimbley egg into it with a silver christening spoon.

"'Tis Grandmuppy Peg's," she said.

Lofty and Eave

"'Twas betwixt a littley's silken gown and a holy card be-scribed with silver songs and godly words. Be yourself chrizzled, Jowge?"

"Christened ... me? No. I don't think my parents believe in God."

"Whatfor does themselves believe in, Jowge?"

"I dunno. I've never asked."

He didn't talk to them about big stuff. If they asked him something, he only ever grunted a few words back. It had never crossed his mind to actually start a conversation with them, but maybe he should. He could think of a lot of things he didn't understand. It would be nice to discuss them.

"What do you believe in, Eave?" he asked.

She didn't give him a straight answer, she just pulled her gloves off, pressed her fingertips together and screwed her eyes shut tight.

"In soil and sea and sky and tree, goodly Goffins does believe."

She opened her eyes "If yourself be wantin' to help, light yonder stove, Jowge."

"OK," said George. "Where are the matches?"

"Doesn't yourself be knowin' how to make fire?" Eave was astonished. "Maybe 'tis because yourself be a Lundiner, Jowge."

But being a city boy was no excuse. George began to regret the days he'd wasted sitting in front of the telly instead of learning how to survive like his ancestors. Yet again he was reminded of his father urging him to join the scouts and how he'd refused because Jermaine said scouts was for losers. But how could knowing how to start a fire without matches make you a loser? It could save your life!

Lofty wandered into the kitchen, fetched an old barley sugar tin from a drawer and pulled up a chair next to George.

"Myneself be in the mood for showin' off some fire-startin' tricks," he said. "Though daresay yourself will soon be raisin' a betterly flame than this old Goffin!"

Lofty seemed to have every confidence in him, unlike his dad. George's dad used to try to teach him things but they were usually things he didn't want to learn, so he didn't listen, then he'd do it wrong and his father would lose his temper and give up.

"My dad never shows me stuff like this," George complained. "He never takes any interest in me."

Lofty took the lid off the barley sugar tin and tapped it on the table.

"Ah, but does yourself be takin' any interest in your pappy?"

"He's not very interesting," scoffed George.

"Nay, your pappy be a hero," insisted Eave. "Himself did save a littley from drowndin' in Ponder's Lake."

She wiped her hands down her front and

disappeared. George knew Ponder's Lake.
It was near Grandma's house. He'd thrown
stones in it; it was pretty deep. "But why has
he never mentioned it?" said George.

"Lionbraves does rarely roar about
themselves," murmured Lofty as Eave
reappeared, waving an old newspaper at
him. There was a photo of George's father
on the front page, looking much younger
than he did now.

"It did happen before yourself
be borned, Jowge,"
said Eave.

Lofty and Eave

The paper was dated 24 January 1978.
George read how Phillip Carruthers, aged
eighteen, had risked his life to rescue five-
year-old Holly Ellis, who had been skating on
the frozen lake and fallen through the ice.

His father had done that! He jumped into
a frozen lake, swam through icy water and
saved a child's life. That took real guts. George
cringed. Only last June, he'd refused to take
part in the school swimming gala because he
reckoned the heated pool was a bit chilly. No
wonder his dad had been disappointed in him.
Lofty tried to cheer him up.

"This Goffin be bettin' yourself does heroic
deeds in yondertimes, Jowge."

"Yay!" said Eave. "Himself be a Carruthers!"

George was so grateful that the Goffins had
such high hopes for him, he was determined
not to be a failure. He'd ask his dad about
joining the scouts, for a start. Maybe he'd
ask his mum for swimming lessons. Karate
lessons. Whatever it took. He was day

dreaming about the heroic deeds he might do when Eave brought him back to reality.

"Hastily, Jowge! Be lightin' myne stove before this Chimbley egg does hatch!"

From Lofty, George learnt that there were several ways to make a fire. The first way was to use a piece of glass to concentrate the sun's rays onto a piece of dry timber. "Myneself does use your Great Grandpappy Sid's monickle for that very purpose," said Lofty, screwing the monacle into his left eye and looming at George "Or else, myneself be usin' this..."

He pulled a serrated knife and a lump of flint out of his pocket and began to saw the blade across the stone.

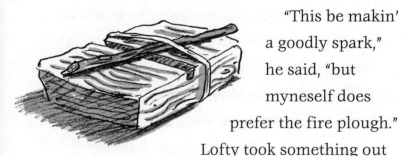

"This be makin' a goodly spark," he said, "but myneself does prefer the fire plough." Lofty took something out of a tin and gave it to George. It was a block of wood with a groove cut in it and there was a stick strapped to it with an elastic band. The idea was to rub the stick in the groove until the friction caused a spark which would then ignite the tinder.

"It does oh-nee take a smincey spark to be cotchin' the tinder a-blaze," Lofty told him.

On Inish Goff, his ancestors used fir cones, powdered fungi and pine needles as tinder,

but Lofty and Eave had to make do with what was available in the attic.

"Us be using woodworm dust," said Lofty, "and feathies plucked from pilloows."

Eave was cutting crusts off the bread which George's mother had thrown out for the birds. The bread was a bit muddy where Lofty had dragged it through a puddle on his fishing line, but having checked for slugs, Eave picked the bits of clover off and spread each slice with honey.

"Once the tinder be a-blaze, us must be feedin' it with fuel," said Lofty.

He reached into the tin and brought out several sticks of artist's charcoal and while George rubbed away with the fire plough, Lofty crumbled the sticks in the bottom of the stove.

"What will you use for fuel when the charcoal runs out?" asked George.

Lofty and Eave

"Animal doin's mixed with leaves. Wood from oak furniture. Clinker from the bunker." Lofty replied.

Grandma Peggy still had a concrete bunker to store coal in, but George's dad was going to get rid of it.

"Grandma won't be having a real fire this winter," said George. "Dad says they're too messy. He wants to put gas fires in."

He promised Lofty he'd collect him some firewood from the park. He was just about to add matches to his list of things to bring them when he raised a spark with the fire plough.

It caught the charcoal which began to

glow. George was beside himself with excitement – like a caveman who'd just discovered fire. It was a first for him. He felt triumphant.

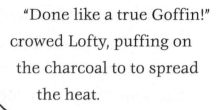

"Done like a true Goffin!" crowed Lofty, puffing on the charcoal to to spread the heat.

When it was hot enough, Eave put the pan on the stove and once the water began to bubble, the Chimbley egg only took a minute to cook.

"How long does a hen's egg take?" asked George.

"Clucky eggs be takin' thrice longer times than Chimbley eggs – but whyfor be yourself askin'? Cookin' be your Muppy's job, nay?"

"Things are going to change," said George. "I'm going to make Grandma Peggy a boiled egg for lunch, with bread and honey. Could I have the basket with the fancy handle back, please?"

Lofty and Eave

Lofty went to fetch it and George looked around for Eave, but she'd disappeared again. He wanted to ask if she'd mind swapping some of her honey for matches, toilet roll and pastry. Just then, she returned with her hands behind her back.

"Please be givin' this to Grandmuppy Peggy," she said.

She handed him a tattered picture book with a dog on the cover. It was the same book he'd seen in the oil painting of the lady reading to a child.

"Thanks. What's special about the book?"

She just smiled and handed him her biggest pot of honey.

"'Tis a Kindness," she said. "Be spreadin' myne honnee thick, Jowge.

He didn't need telling twice. He would spread honey and kindness as thickly as he could. He wasn't Weedy G, he was a Carruthers! His ancestors were fearless explorers, soldiers and heroes. He was proud of them; the last thing he wanted to do was let them down.

His parents were still out, so George left the Goffins and went back downstairs to make himself busy in the kitchen. He put an egg on to boil, buttered some bread and spread it generously with Eave's honey. Then he arranged everything in the fancy basket, tucked the picture book under his arm and went to see Grandma.

Lofty and Eave

He knocked on
her door. She was
awake, but she didn't
smile when she saw
him. He hoped it
was because she
was wearing her
spare set of teeth
and not because she
didn't want to talk
to him. Maybe she'd
forgotten what fun
they'd had earlier.
He sat by her bed
while she knocked
the top off the egg.
He hoped the yolk
wasn't too hard.

"Not bad," she
said. "You might have
cut the crusts off the
bread though."

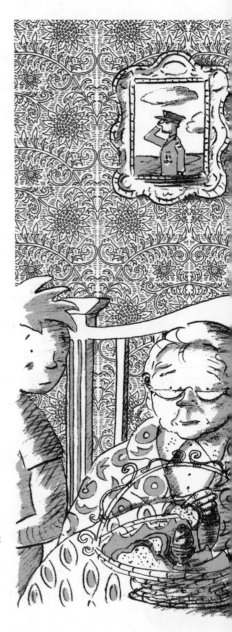

She still didn't smile but as soon as she tasted the honey her whole face lit up. For a few seconds, George could see the sunny little girl she still was under her wrinkles.

"Shop-bought, was it?" she asked.

George shook his head.

"Didn't think so." She grinned. "Lovely! What else have you got there, boy? A book?"

George gave it to her. It was called *Buster Brown, His Dog, Tige, and their Jolly Times*.

"Thought you might like to see it," he said.

Grandma turned the pages slowly and as she looked at the pictures, her eyes misted over.

"This was your Grandpa Gordon's," she said. "His mother used to read it to him when he was little. And I used to read it to your dad when he was little – ha!"

She shook her head as if she found it impossible to believe that George's father had ever been little. "It seems so long ago ... a lifetime!" she said, fumbling for her glasses.

"Shall I read it to you?" asked George.

Grandma nodded and as he read, she began to doze off, but she was smiling. Halfway through, she woke up, patted his arm and said he reminded her of Grandpa Gordon.

"I miss him," she said. "One of the best, he was. It's no fun being on your own, boy."

George squeezed her hand.

"You're not on your own though, are you—?"

George could have kicked himself. He'd almost told her about Lofty and Eave.

"What I mean is," George started again, "now that we're all living under the same roof, we could be friends, couldn't we, Grandma?"

"Friends," murmured Grandma. "Under the same roof? I get you."

Their eyes met briefly and in that moment, George suspected that she knew about the Goffins, but he couldn't prove it.

"Grand ... ma," he said. "Us could be allies ... yay?"

She blinked at him innocently.

"What kind of funny talk is that?" she said. "I don't know what you're on about."

She wiped the egg yolk off her dressing gown and told him to put the crusts on the bird table.

George noticed that she'd
left rather a lot of
bread on them.

"Shall I put the
crusts in the
basket?" he asked.
"The one with the
long handle?"

"You can if you want. It can't do any harm,
can it?" She lay back on her pillow and
chuckled. "We shall have jolly times, boy. Like
Buster Brown and his dog. Finish the story!"

But that story was just the beginning.

Fun and Games
in book 2

out now!

The summer holidays are flying by for George and his friends the Goffins. Being left alone with grumpy Grandma isn't so bad when Lofty and Eave show him how to play Spillikins, marbles and the twigaloo!

Is there a Goffin in *your* attic?